A Fine
St. Patrick's Day

by Susan Wojciechowski ✤ illustrated by Tom Curry

Random House 🏠 New York

www.randomhouse.com/kids

Library of Congress Cataloging-in-Publication Data
Wojciechowski, Susan.
A fine St. Patrick's Day / by Susan Wojciechowski ;
illustrated by Tom Curry. — 1st ed.   p.   cm.
SUMMARY: Two towns, Tralee and Tralah, compete in an annual St. Patrick's Day
decorating contest which Tralah boastfully always wins, but when their hearts are put
to the test by a little man with pointed ears, Tralee wins with no effort at all.
ISBN 0-375-82386-7 (trade) — ISBN 0-375-92386-1 (lib. bdg.)
[1. St. Patrick's Day—Fiction. 2. Competition (Psychology)—Fiction.
3. Leprechauns—Fiction.]
I. Curry, Tom, ill. II. Title.
PZ7.W8183 Fi 2004   [E]—dc21   2002011684

MANUFACTURED IN CHINA 10 9 8 7 6 5 4 3 2 1 First Edition

To Christian, with so much love—
this one's for you!
—S. W.

To Miss Emily O'Fallon.
'Tis a fine granddaughter.
—T. C.

For as far back as anyone could remember, the towns of Tralee and Tralah had been rivals. Every year on St. Patrick's Day, they held a contest to see which town could decorate best for the holiday. And though the people of Tralee tried their hardest, they never won. The prize, a golden trophy in the shape of a shamrock, was always awarded to Tralah.

Each year, when the winner was announced by the official county judge, the people of Tralee sighed and said, "Next year we'll win, to be sure."

The people of Tralah laughed at them. "No you won't. You have always lost, and you always will," they said.

One year the mayor of Tralee rang the bell in the town square, calling all the townspeople to gather. When everyone was there, he said, "Little Fiona Riley, though she's but a wee lass of six, has come up with a fine idea for this year's contest. We'll win, to be sure, but only if everyone agrees to it." Little Fiona's plan was to paint everything in the town bright green.

"'Tis a fine idea," said Emily O'Fallon. "But will all of our homes be painted green?"

"Yes," said the mayor.

"'Tis surely a fine idea," said Reverend Flaherty. "But will even the churches be green?"

"Yes."

"'Tis a most excellent idea," said Brogan O'Neill, the school principal. "But will the school be green?"

"Yes," said the mayor. "Everything, right down to the wee doghouses, will be painted green."

"Except for the mailboxes," said Mr. Root, the postmaster. "They are government property."

"And the fire hydrants," added Captain Blazes, the fire chief. "They must stay yellow to be seen."

A hush came over the crowd as the townspeople thought about the plan. When the mayor asked how many wanted to paint the town green, everyone shouted and cheered and whooped and hollered and said, "'Tis a fine idea. This year we'll win, to be sure!" They agreed that little Fiona Riley's name should be engraved on the trophy.

The people of Tralee bought painters' hats and coveralls. They bought brushes and rollers. They rummaged through basements and sheds for ladders and buckets. And little Fiona was allowed to choose the shade of green they would use: Emerald Isle, Limerick Lime, or Galway Green. Fiona chose Limerick Lime. Mr. and Mrs. Kelly, who owned the hardware store, ordered hundreds and hundreds of gallons of Limerick Lime paint.

Meanwhile, the people of Tralah were planning, too. They decided to cut shamrocks from green cardboard, sprinkle them with glitter, and hang them from every branch of every tree in town.

On the day before St. Patrick's Day, as everyone
in Tralee and Tralah was busy working on decorations,
a little man on a large horse came galloping across
the meadow. He wore red trousers, a brown leather
apron, and boots decorated with gold bells. His beard
came down to his stomach. Pointed ears stuck out
beneath the brim of his hat. His horse had long satin
ribbons braided into its mane.

The man turned toward Tralah and stopped at Mrs. Donegal's house at the edge of town. He pounded on the front door. Mrs. Donegal, scissors in hand, answered.

Frantically the little man asked, "Begging your pardon, can you help me? I was leading my cows across the river and, sure and begorra, they are stuck in the mud!"

"You picked the wrong day to ask for help," said Mrs. Donegal sharply. "I'm cutting shamrocks." She shut the door in his face.

The stranger hurried to the next house. When Mr. O'Leary answered the door, the little man asked, "Begging your pardon, can you help me? I was leading my cows across the river and, sure and begorra, they are stuck in the mud."

"Away with you," said Mr. O'Leary. "I'm busy cutting string for our shamrocks."

"The river is cold. My cows won't last much longer, to be sure," said the stranger. But Mr. O'Leary had shut the door and gone back to measuring his lengths of string.

At the third house the little man asked again, "Begging your pardon, can you help me? I was leading my cows across the river and, sure and begorra, they are stuck in the mud."

The McLeans, their hands covered with glitter and glue, looked annoyed. "Don't you know what day this is?" Mrs. McLean asked. "We're busy getting ready to beat Tralee in the contest."

At every house the stranger was turned away.

Finally, he crossed the field into Tralee. At the first house he came upon, he asked, "Begging your pardon, can you help me? I was leading my cows across the river and, sure and begorra, they are stuck in the mud."

Mary Kate Driscoll was on her ladder, paintbrush in hand. Her coveralls were splattered with Limerick Lime paint. Her face was smudged with Limerick Lime blotches. She climbed down and looked at the little man. She looked up at her house. She scratched her head. "Follow me," Mary Kate said.

She ran to the town square and rang the bell until the townspeople came, wearing coveralls and painters' hats.

The little man yelled out to the crowd, "Begging your pardon, can you help me? I was leading my cows across the river and, sure and begorra, they are stuck in the mud."

"But what about our painting?" someone shouted.

"What about the contest?" called another voice. "This is the year we'll win, to be sure."

"What about the trophy?" a third person called out.

Little Fiona Riley was sitting atop her father's shoulders, listening. She looked down at the people all splattered with Limerick Lime paint. She thought about the golden trophy. She thought about having her name engraved on it. Finally she called out, in a voice loud and clear, "But what about the cows? We need to help the cows."

A hush came over the crowd as everyone considered what little Fiona had said.

"'Tis a fine idea," said Emily O'Fallon.

"'Tis surely a fine idea," said Reverend Flaherty.

"'Tis a most excellent idea," said Brogan O'Neill.

When the mayor took a vote of how many people wanted to help the stranger, every hand went up. The crowd shouted and cheered and whooped and hollered.

All the people of Tralee headed for the river—the children, the old folks, and families with babies. They went in wagons, on bicycles, and on foot. As they crossed the meadow, they heard the sound of cowbells.

And when they reached the river, sure and begorra, there were the little man's cows, stuck in the mud.

Everyone pushed and pulled and tugged. One by one, the cows were freed from the mud at the bottom of the river.

The sun had long set by the time the people of Tralee got back to their homes and fell into bed, tired and wet.

"Ah, well, next year we'll win, to be sure," said the mayor to his wife as he sank into a deep, snoring sleep.

The following morning, the people of Tralee woke to the sound
of the bell ringing in the town square. They ran outside in their
pajamas and nightgowns, and in the case of old Mr. Murphy, bright
red long underwear. What they saw was so incredible they could
barely believe their eyes. Every inch of Tralee was green—sparkling,

shimmering, glimmering, glorious green—from the wee doghouses
to the tall spire of the church (except for the mailboxes, being
government property, and the fire hydrants, which remained yellow
so they could be seen). The people of Tralee shouted and cheered
and whooped and hollered, "This year we'll win, to be sure!"

And they did. When the official county judge rode through the two towns, he declared Tralee to be the winner and handed the mayor the prize. The trophy case in the town hall was no longer empty. It now held one golden shamrock, which would soon be engraved with little Fiona's name.

As the St. Patrick's Day supper of lamb and boiled potatoes was set out in the town hall, the mayor asked some of the townspeople to find the stranger and invite him to the party. They rode across the meadow, beyond the river, and as far as the peat bog, but they could not find the little man or his cows. All they found was a single cowbell. It was made of shining gold.

And though the people of Tralee passed the golden cowbell from hand to hand and talked throughout supper about the glimmering, glorious green miracle, no one could account for what had happened. All they could remember was the tinkling sound of the little man's boots and the beautiful ribbons in his horse's mane. Little Fiona Riley remembered that when the man thanked her at the river, he said, "You have already won."

As the sun began to sink behind the hills, the town slowly faded back to its real colors. "'Twas a fine St. Patrick's Day," the mayor said. He took the golden shamrock from the trophy case and put it into little Fiona Riley's hands. Everyone shouted and cheered and whooped and hollered.

The following year, when it came time to plan how to win the contest, little Fiona Riley, though she was but a wee lass of seven, had an idea. When the idea was put to a vote, everyone shouted and cheered and whooped and hollered.

That St. Patrick's Day and every year afterward, though they would take the shamrock and the golden cowbell out of the trophy case and polish them, the people of Tralee would no longer compete with Tralah to win another trophy. They would decorate their town and share a meal of lamb and boiled potatoes simply for the joy of it.

'Twas a fine idea, to be sure.